To my aunts and uncles, Selma and Herman Krauss
and Edna and Albert Rettig: May your candles
burn bright! —L. K. M.

For Dr. Désiré Amsellem, who was a very dear friend.

And many thanks to The Museum of Art and
History of Judaism in Paris. —E. S.

Text © 2010 by Laura Krauss Melmed.
Illustrations © 2010 by Elisabeth Schlossberg.

Library of Congress Cataloging-in-Publication Data
Melmed, Laura Krauss.
Eight winter nights : a family Hanukkah book / by Laura Krauss Melmed ;
illustrated by Elisabeth Schlossberg.
p. cm.
Summary: Short verses describe symbols, foods, and family fun associated with the
festival of Hanukkah. Includes facts about the history and traditions.
ISBN 978-0-8118-5552-5
[1. Stories in rhyme. 2. Hanukkah—Fiction. 3. Judaism—Customs and practices—
Fiction.] I. Schlossberg, Elisabeth, ill. II. Title.
PZ8.3.M55155Eig 2010
[E]—dc22
2009019574

Book design by Molly Baker and Amelia Anderson.
Typeset in Esta and Silent Movie.
The illustrations in this book were rendered in pencil and pastels.

Manufactured by Toppan Leefung, Da Ling Shan Town, Dongguan, China, in July 2010.

1 3 5 7 9 10 8 6 4 2

This product conforms to CPSIA 2008.

Chronicle Books LLC
680 Second Street, San Francisco, California 94107

www.chroniclekids.com

Eight Winter Nights

A Family Hanukkah Book

by Laura Krauss Melmed

illustrated by Elisabeth Schlossberg

chronicle books san francisco

Getting Ready

Each year we take eight winter nights
To kindle our menorah's lights.
Tick-tock! Don't be late!
We're getting set to celebrate!

Polishing
the Menorah

Rub-a-dub up
Rub-a-dub down
'Til our menorah
Shines like a crown.

Colored Candles

Red as a fire truck, blue as the sky,
Yellow as wings on a butterfly,
Green as a grasshopper, pink as a bow,
Orange as apricots, white as snow.
Pick the candles you like the best
To light tonight. We'll save the rest.

First Night

Now the sun has gone away
And stars are coming out to play
It's time to start our holiday!

The First Candle

Outside there's snowy blow-y weather,
But here at home we're snug together—
Daddy, Baby, Grandpa, Brother,
Sister holding hands with Mother—
All watching on this special night
As Grandma sets one flame alight.

The Ninth Candle

The shammes candle stands up straight,
A servant and quite proud of it.
He always is the first one lit
And then he lights the other eight.

Second Night
We'll choose two candles,
Light the menorah,
Turn up the music
And dance the hora.

Hanukkah Rock

Sway to the music,
Bounce to the beat,
Feel the rockin' rhythm
In your feet, feet, feet,
Give a little shimmy,
Prance a little prance,
Whirl around and twirl around
And dance, dance, dance.

Third Night

At our window we will show
How warmly our three candles glow.

The Storyteller

The children sit on Grandpa's knee
To learn of Judah Maccabee
And why each year we tell the story
Of those ancient deeds of glory.

Fourth Night

Tonight is a light-four-flames night.
Tonight is a fun-and-games night.

Dreidel Game

I'm a little dreidel,
Watch me spin,
Nun, *gimel*, *hey*, and *shin*.
The way I fall,
Tells who will win.

Dreidel Chase

I had a little dreidel,
I made it out of clay,
But Baby grabbed my dreidel,
And now I cannot play.
Let's catch that naughty baby—
OOPS! Baby got away!

Fifth Night

It's SO hard to wait
'Til the cousins arrive
To help light the candles
On night number five.

They're Here!

BRR-RRING goes the doorbell
And in rush the cousins—
Wild ones, noisy ones,
There must be dozens!
What a commotion, what a delight
When cousins come calling this
Hanukkah night!

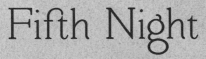

Golden Coins

Chocolate coins! Hanukkah *gelt*!
Munch them fast before they melt!

Sixth Night

Sizzling latkes, such a treat,
With applesauce so cool and sweet,
Let's light six candles; then we'll eat.

Latkes . . .

Latkes in the frying pan,
Latkes on your plate,
Latkes for the family,
Who ate and ate and ate.

...and Applesauce!

Applesauce, applesauce on your nose.
Applesauce, applesauce on your toes.
Applesauce, applesauce on your thumb.
Applesauce, applesauce in your tummy-tum-tum.
Applesauce, applesauce, we like it best.
Applesauce, applesauce, east to west.
Applesauce, applesauce, north to south.
Here comes the applesauce—open your mouth!

Seventh Night

Seven candles shining bright
Send all the world a gift of light.

Opening Presents

Sister got a painting set,
Brother got a model jet,
Baby got a teddy bear
And sat it on her potty chair.

Tzedakah

We save our coins up in a jar
To help our neighbors, near and far.

Eighth Night

Eight blazing candles stand up tall
On this, the brightest night of all.
Though Hanukkah ends now it's true,
Next year we'll celebrate anew.

A Lucky Number

$$
\begin{aligned}
& 1 \\
+ & 2 \\
+ & 3 \\
+ & 4 \\
+ & 5 \\
+ & 6 \\
+ & 7 \\
+ & 8 \\
\end{aligned}
$$

Makes 36,
And here's the wonder—
36 is a lucky number!

Good Night

The snow is white.
The stars are bright.
The family is sleeping tight,
Wrapped in dreams
Of candlelight.

Hanukkah

About two thousand years ago, the Jewish people were ruled by a cruel foreign king named Antiochus. He would not let them practice their religion and forced them to bow down to statues placed inside their holy temple. Out of fear, many people obeyed. But a small band of fighters led by Judah Maccabee would not give in. They battled Antiochus's army for three years and finally won. When they reclaimed the temple, they found that the eternal lamp, meant to be kept burning at all times, had gone out. According to tradition, there was only enough special oil to relight the lamp for one day. But the oil burned for eight days and nights, the time needed to prepare more oil.

Hanukkah celebrates the triumph of freedom and the miracle of the lights. Families light candles in a holder called a menorah, adding a candle for each of the eight nights. Foods fried in oil, such as potato latkes and jelly donuts, are eaten during Hanukkah.

Hanukkah Traditions

The menorah is a holder for the eight candles of Hanukkah plus the shammes candle, which sits apart from the other candles and is used to light them. Each night of Hanukkah, another candle is lit, until on the last night there are nine candles burning.

A dreidel is a spinning top with a Hebrew letter on each of four sides. The letters—*shin*, *hey*, *gimel*, and *nun*—are the first four letters of the Hebrew words "A Great Miracle Happened Here." By spinning the dreidel, players win candy or pennies in a game of chance.

Gelt are coins, real or chocolate, given to children during Hanukkah.

The hora is an Israeli circle dance based on a folk dance from Romania.

Latkes are crispy potato pancakes that are traditional Hanukkah treats. Foods fried in oil are often eaten during Hanukkah because oil is such an important part of the holiday's history. Latkes are usually eaten with applesauce or sour cream.

Tzedakah is the practice of giving aid, assistance, and/or money to the poor and needy or to other worthy causes. The Hebrew word *tzedakah* actually means righteousness, justice, or fairness. Traditional Jewish homes may keep a tzedakah box for collecting coins. During Hanukkah, since children usually receive gifts, some families perform tzedakah to teach that giving is as important as receiving.

In Jewish lore, each Hebrew letter is assigned a number. The word *chai* meaning "life" or "good luck," has a value of 18; any multiple of 18 is commonly considered a lucky number.